FIREMAN SAM
AND THE BARBECUE

story by Diane Wilmer
illustrations by The County Studio

GUILD PUBLISHING

LONDON · NEW YORK · SYDNEY · TORONTO

Station Officer Steele was planning to hold an Open Day at Pontypandy Fire Station.

"We'll have it on Saturday afternoon and invite everyone in Pontypandy to come and look round the Fire Station," he said.

"I'll park Jupiter on the drive," said Fireman Sam. "Then people can have a really good look at her."

"And we'll take our visitors all over the Station," said Station Officer Steele. "So they can see for themselves just how well organised we are."

"Will you take them *everywhere*?" asked Elvis Cridlington.

"Everywhere!" said Station Officer Steele.

"What, even the kitchen?" asked Elvis.

"Certainly," answered Station Officer Steele. "Visitors can look in our kitchen if they want to."

"But it's a tip!" cried Elvis.

"Yes, it is," agreed Fireman Sam.

"Then you must clean it up," said Station Officer Steele.

"But if I clean it up I won't be able to cook anything in it for our visitors," said Elvis.

"Why ever not?" asked Station Officer Steele.

"Because as soon as I start cooking I'll make a terrible mess all over again," said Elvis.

"Dear, oh dear," said Station Officer Steele. "We can't have our visitors coming all the way up the hill from Pontypandy and not offer them a bite to eat or a cup of tea, can we?"

"I know what we can do to keep the kitchen clean," said Fireman Sam. "We can set up a barbecue in the garden. Then everybody will be happy."

"Brill!" cried Elvis. "I'll cook sausages and burgers and we could ask all our visitors to bring along a little something – a chop or a piece of chicken – anything they fancy."

"That's a jolly good idea," said Station Officer Steele. "Right men! At the double! To work!"

Fireman Sam asked Norman, Sarah and James to take
invitations to the people of Pontypandy.

**PONTYPANDY FIRE STATION
OPEN DAY
Saturday 2–7 o'clock
Grand Barbecue
Contributions for the barbecue gratefully accepted**

"Oooh! Thank you very much," said Dilys. "I'll certainly
come for a look round and I'll bring a nice tomato salad to
go with the barbecue."

"Bellissima!" cried Bella. "I'd love to come, and I'll bring along one of my beautiful Italian salads. Beans and olives with garlic and oil. Mmmmm ... delicioso!"

Trevor Evans said he'd be there anyway, helping out as a part-time fireman.

"I'll bring along a crunchy cucumber salad," he said. "Fresh vegetables from my garden, you can't beat them."

"Everybody's bringing boring salads," moaned Norman. "You can't grill a cucumber!"

The morning of the Open Day was very busy. Fireman Sam washed down Jupiter then polished her until she shone. Station Officer Steele swept the driveway and tidied his office.

But poor Elvis was in a spin. He was trying to tidy the kitchen *and* prepare the barbecue, but he was making a mess of both.

"Calm down, Elvis," said Trevor. He helped Elvis mop the kitchen floor, then went outside to decorate the Fire Station and the garden with bright flags and pretty streamers.

"Well done, men," said Station Officer Steele, as soon as he was ready. "The Station looks magnificent. Now, let's get ourselves tidied up before our visitors arrive."

He, Fireman Sam and Trevor Evans went upstairs to change. But outside poor Elvis was still struggling to get the barbecue ready.

"Oh my!" he flapped. "I'd better get the fire lit first, I think."

But just as he started to light the barbecue, he remembered he hadn't defrosted the burgers.

"Help!" he cried and ran back into the kitchen, but he was in such a rush he sent all the sausages and bread rolls flying onto the floor.

"This is too much," spluttered Elvis as he fell headlong over the slippery sausages.

"Come along now," boomed Station Officer Steele, who was looking very smart in his best uniform. "Just pull yourself together, Cridlington, and get this barbecue under control."

"I'm trying, Sir," gasped Elvis. "I really am trying!"

"Everything will be tickety-boo if you stay cool, calm and collected, just like me!" said Station Officer Steele. "Shape up, Elvis. I can see some visitors coming up the hill."

The first to arrive were Dilys Price and her son, Norman.
  "Oh! Can I help you cook the burgers?" asked Norman.
  "Not now Norman," said Elvis. "I've only just lit the fire.
Go and have a look round, why don't you?"
  Station Officer Steele was trying to gather together a
group for his "Official Fire Station Tour".

"Come along now," he called to Norman but Dilys caught hold of Norman's arm.

"You follow me, my lovely," she whispered. "We'll have a quick peep round on our own."

"But I don't think we're allowed to look upstairs, Mam," said Norman.

"We won't be long," said Dilys. "We'll just pop up and have a peep, then come down again. After all, it is Open Day."

Upstairs they found hats, boots and jackets, and a couple of
beds that the firemen used when they were working on
nightshifts.

"Not very interesting," grumbled Norman.

Then he spotted the pole.

"Oh Mam!" he gasped. "Look at that."

"Now Norman!" cried Dilys. "Don't you go..." but it was
too late. With a leap Norman grabbed the pole and
disappeared.

"WHHHHEEE – – – AAAAAAAAAAHHHH!"

"Come on, Mam," he shouted from the bottom of the pole. "It's brill!"

"Don't be daft, Norman," cried Dilys. "I can't go whizzing down poles at my age."

But just then she heard footsteps coming up the stairs.

"My goodness! I'd better get out of here," thought Dilys and she leapt for the pole.

"WHEEEEE – – – AAAAAAAHHHHH!" she cried and landed right on top of Elvis who was running through with a tray of sausages for the barbecue.

SPLAT! What a mess!

Norman who had run up the stairs to have another go, looked down at Dilys and Elvis and started to giggle.

"Cor Mam," he snorted. "You won't half cop it!"

Elvis and Dilys stood up and tried to untangle their legs and feet from the string of sausages.

"Gosh, Mrs Price," gasped Elvis. "You gave me such a fright!"

He picked up his tray and ran outside wiping the sausages clean on his jacket. "Good job we washed the floor this morning," he muttered.

Inside the Fire Station Norman had finished whizzing down the pole and was looking round the empty engine shed.

"Now Norman, my lovely," cooed Dilys. "Don't go fiddling with anything else. We're in enough trouble already. Do you hear me, now?"

But it was too late.

Naughty Norman had spotted a big red button on the wall.

"Ooh, Mam, what's this for?" he asked, reaching towards it.

"NO! Norman, don't!" cried Dilys, but . . .

RIIIIIIIIIIIIIIIIIIIIIIING!

"Action stations!" shouted Station Officer Steele and he ran across the garden towards Jupiter who was parked on the drive.

Fireman Sam and Trevor came rushing up, and Elvis left his barbecue just as the sausages and burgers were beginning to brown nicely on the top.

"EMERGENCY!" he shouted and jumped into Jupiter with a knife and fork in his hand.

"All present and correct, Sir!" said Fireman Sam.

"Right men," said Station Officer Steele. "Now, where's the fire?"

The firemen looked at each other.

"STOP!" cried Dilys, running up. "Don't go. My Norman rang the bell. It was a mistake!"

Station Officer Steele jumped off Jupiter and glared at naughty Norman.

"Now then young man. How many times have you been told not to touch things which are none of your business?" he asked.

Norman looked at his feet and wriggled about.

"I'm sorry," he said. "But it was all Mam's fault, see. She took me upstairs and slid down your pole and . . ."

"Oooh! You bad boy, Norman!" interrupted Dilys going as red as a tomato. "You slid down the pole first."

"Well, it sounds to me as if you've both been up to no good," said Station Officer Steele.

Fireman Sam was trying hard not to laugh. The thought of Dilys whizzing down the pole gave him terrible giggles.

"Maybe you should join the Fire Service, eh Dilys?" he grinned. "Anyway, no harm done, so let's get back to the barbecue, shall we?"

"The barbecue!" shouted Elvis. "It'll be ruined!"

He shot across the lawn but it was too late. The sausages and burgers were burnt to a crisp.

"I don't believe it," wailed Elvis. "Now what shall we eat?"

"We'll just have to cook the food our visitors have brought," said Fireman Sam.

"Good idea, Fireman Sam," said Station Officer Steele.
"Right everybody, let's see what you've got."

"Beautiful Italian salad," said Bella.

"Tasty tomato salad," said Dilys.

"Crunchy cucumber salad," said Trevor.

"But we can't barbecue salad," said Elvis.

"Huh! That's what *I* said in the first place," said Norman.

"You keep quiet, my boy," said Station Officer Steele.
"You caused all this trouble in the first place. We'll just
have to eat all these lovely salads."

Everybody felt sorry for poor Elvis. He'd spent so much
time and trouble getting the barbecue ready and now it
was a disaster. They all tucked into the salads and tried to
look cheerful.

"Well, *I'm* not eating salad," insisted Norman. "I want a burger, with lots of ketchup and chilli sauce. Mmmmm, that would be good!"

"Hush now, my lovely," hissed Dilys. "You can't have a burger now, but your Mam will make you one later."

Suddenly Sarah and James came running up the drive.

"Hello! Hello!" they called. "Sorry we're late, but we ordered these burgers from the butcher and we had to queue up for ages."

"BURGERS!" yelled Norman.

"Yes, lots," they said and plonked a great big box of burgers in the middle of the table.

"Yippee!" cheered Norman. "Bags I have the first one!"

Elvis cooked the juicy burgers then put them in warm buns speckled with sesame seeds.

"Here Norman," he said. "Help yourself to sauces."

"YUMMMEEE!" grinned Norman and squirted a big dollop of ketchup on the burger and then a huge blob of chilli sauce.

"Hey, Norman," warned Elvis. "Take it easy with that chilli sauce, it's dynamite!"

"Huh! It won't be too hot for me," boasted Norman and he took an enormous bite of the big, juicy burger.

"YAAAAAA–AHHHH!" he roared. His eyes filled with tears and nearly popped out of his head.

"I'm on fire … water! water!" he bellowed.

Before anyone could stop him he'd rushed over to the fire bucket and stuck his head right in it.

"GLUG! GLUG! GLUG!" he burbled.

"That should cool him off a bit," grinned Fireman Sam.

"Yes," laughed Trevor. "He's looking positively chilly now!"

FIREMAN SAM SAYS
a barbecue can be fun, but a grown-up
should light it and keep an eye on
it at all times.

This edition published 1989 by Guild Publishing
by arrangement with William Heinemann Ltd

First published 1988 by William Heinemann
Fireman Sam © 1985 Prism Art & Design Ltd
Text © 1988 William Heinemann Ltd
Illustrations © 1988 William Heinemann Ltd
All rights reserved

Based on the animation series produced by Bumper Films
for S4C – Channel 4 Wales – and Prism Art & Design Ltd

Original idea by Dave Gingell and Dave Jones, assisted
by Mike Young

Characters created by Rob Lee

Printed in Great Britain by
Springbourne Press Ltd